and the Fire Engine Parade

For Annelise, Ashley, Helen, and Cherylyn—P.J.
For Tanner Paxton who loves fire trucks—M.J.

For information contact:
MONDO Publishing
980 Avenue of the Americas
New York, NY 10018
Visit our web site at http://www.mondopub.com
Printed in the United States of America
02 03 04 05 06 07 08 HC 9 8 7 6 5 4 3 2 1
02 03 04 05 06 07 08 PB 9 8 7 6 5 4 3 2 1
ISBN 1-59034-192-9 (hardcover)   ISBN 1-59034-036-1 (pbk.)

Designed by Edward Miller

Library of Congress Cataloging-in-Publication Data

Jane, Pamela
    Milo and the fire engine parade / by Pamela Jane ; illustrated by Meredith Johnson.
       p. cm.
    Summary: Milo thinks he is going to miss the fire engine parade, but when his dog
Wolf escapes from the yard, they both end up in the middle of things.
    ISBN 1-59034-036-1 (pbk.) -- ISBN 1-59034-192-9
    [1. Parades--Fiction. 2. Dog--Fiction. 3. Fire engines--Fiction.] I. Johnson, Meredith,
ill. II.Title.

PZ7 .J213 Mi 2002
[E]--dc21   2001058710

Milo

and the Fire Engine Parade

by Pamela Jane

Illustrated by Meredith Johnson

Milo sat on the porch with his big sister, Sam. The Fire Engine Parade was about to start over on Main Street, but Milo and Sam couldn't go.

"It's all because of Wolf," said Sam. Wolf was Milo's dog. He had a way of getting Milo into trouble.

That morning Sam and Milo had left the gate open. Wolf got out. He chased the paperboy and ate Mrs. May's newspaper—for the third time that week!

Milo and Sam were grounded—again.
So was Wolf. They couldn't go anywhere,
not even to the parade.

"That dog of yours is nothing but trouble!" said Sam.

Milo said nothing. He loved Wolf, but he hated missing the parade.

"Listen!" said Sam. "The parade is starting!"

Milo could hear the roar of the fire engines and the cheering crowd.

Wolf barked loudly. He loved the shiny
red fire engines. Well, he loved chasing
them!

Milo climbed up to his tree house. Maybe he could see the fire trucks over the treetops. But all Milo could see from his tree house was Wolf. He was running down the street to the parade!

Milo forgot all about being grounded.
He slid down from the tree house and
raced after Wolf.

"Wolf, come back!" Milo shouted.

Wolf just ran faster.

Wolf ran under an ice cream cart. Milo tried to grab him, but he slipped on an ice cream cone and . . .

BANG! Milo knocked over the ice cream cart.

The ice cream cart tipped over the soda
stand . . .

and the soda stand sent the fruit cart flying!

The Fire Engine Parade came to a stop. "Uh-oh!" said the fire chief. "Main Street is blocked. We'll have to go down Bacon Street."

Milo sat down on the curb as an old-time fire engine went by.

The firefighters were tossing candy to the boys and girls.

Milo jumped up to catch a piece of
candy and bumped right into a firefighter!

The firefighter smiled. She pulled a
T-shirt over Milo's head.

FUTURE FIREFIGHTER

Just then, Wolf barked and pulled Milo away. Wolf ran down the street, chasing a shiny new fire engine. Milo ran along right behind him.

The fire engine stopped at the corner.
Wolf ran up to it, barking and barking.

"Would you two like a ride?" asked
the firefighter.

The firefighter pulled Milo up onto the truck. Then he put a fire helmet on Milo's head! Wolf jumped up and sat next to Milo.

29

Milo's friends ran beside the fire
engine. They shouted and cheered all
the way to the firehouse.

"Milo, guess what happened!" yelled
Sam when Milo got home later. "The
fire engine parade came right past our
house . . ."

". . . and you and Wolf missed the whole thing!"